JENNIFER LAWRENCE
MOVIE STAR

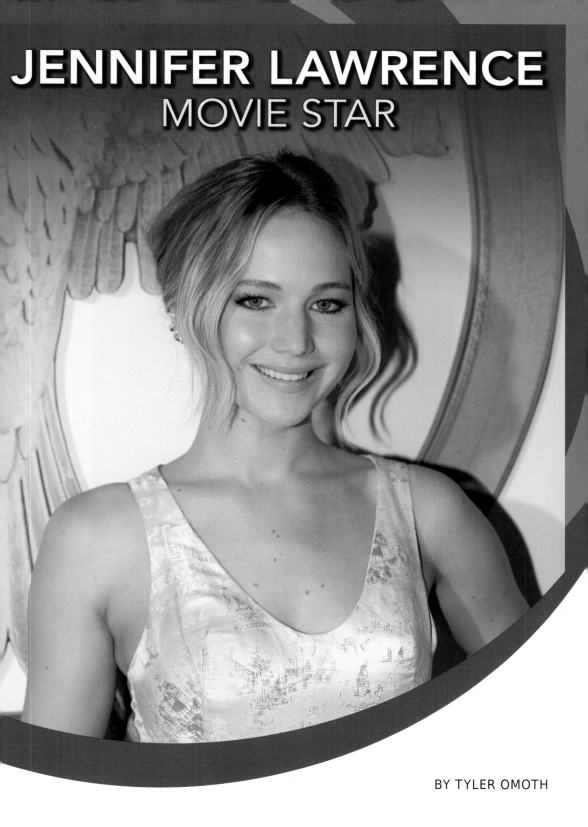

BY TYLER OMOTH

Published by The Child's World®
1980 Lookout Drive • Mankato, MN 56003-1705
800-599-READ • www.childsworld.com

Photographs ©: Matt Sayles/Invision/AP Images, cover, 1; Shutterstock Images, 5;
Chris Pizzello/AP Images, 6, 10; Andrew Medichini/AP Images, 8; Twentieth Century
Fox/Marvel Entertainment/TSG Entertainment/Bad Hat Harry Productions/Album/
Newscom, 13; Joe Seer/Shutterstock Images, 14; Color Force/Lionsgate/Studio
Babelsberg/Close Murray/Album/Newscom, 17; Ga Fullner/Shutterstock Images, 18;
Helga Esteb/Shutterstock Images, 20

ISBN 9781503819948
LCCN 2016960919

Printed in the United States of America
PA02335

ABOUT THE AUTHOR

Tyler Omoth has written more than 30 books for kids, covering a wide variety
of topics. He has also published poetry and award-winning short stories.
He loves sports and new adventures. Tyler currently lives in sunny Brandon,
Florida, with his wife, Mary.

TABLE OF
CONTENTS

FAST FACTS

Name
- Jennifer Shrader Lawrence

Birthdate
- August 15, 1990

Birthplace
- Indian Hills, Kentucky

Fun Trivia
- As a young girl, Jennifer enjoyed playing parts in local church plays, but she never gave any serious thought to acting.
- Jennifer **auditioned** for the part of Bella Swan in the *Twilight* series but lost out to Kristen Stewart.
- In 2016, Jennifer was the highest-paid actress in Hollywood, taking home more than $46 million dollars.
- Jennifer went deaf in one ear for months because of an accident with a water jet during *The Hunger Games: Catching Fire*.

CARTOON NETWORK
TCM
TURNER CLASSIC MOVIES
CNN
tbs
TNT
truTV

Chapter 1

DISCOVERED ON THE STREET

In 2011, Jennifer Lawrence waited for her turn to audition for a movie role that she wanted badly. She had read the books that the movie was based on. She knew the movie series would be amazing.

When the **producer** told her it was her turn to act the part of Katniss Everdeen, Jennifer took the stage. She would be performing a scene where Katniss says good-bye to her little sister. Jennifer poured all of her emotion into the role. When she finished, she looked up. Some of the people watching had tears in their eyes. That's when she knew she had nailed it.

◄ **Jennifer Lawrence attends a party in 2008, shortly before her 18th birthday.**

▲ Jennifer poses with cast members of one of the first movies she appeared in.

Jennifer was raised on a horse farm in Kentucky. She sometimes acted in local plays. But she thought she might be a doctor when she grew up. When Jennifer was 14, she visited New York City with her family. A talent **agent** saw her on the street and asked if he could take her picture. After snapping the photo, he got her family's contact information. When Jennifer got back to her home in Kentucky, the phone began to ring. Agents had seen her photo, and they wanted her to go back to New York to be a model.

But Jennifer decided she wanted to act. She said she would only work with an agent who would allow her to follow that dream. With her agent's help, she started to find work. She appeared next to a giant talking cheeseburger in a commercial for Burger King. She landed a role as a rebellious teenager in the comedy *The Bill Engvall Show*. Jennifer also had a few parts in small **indie movies**. She was still waiting for her big break. She wouldn't have to wait long.

Chapter 2

A STAR IS BORN

In early 2011, Jennifer sat nervously in a crowded theater. Hollywood's biggest stars were there. It was the 2011 **Academy Awards**, and Jennifer had been **nominated** for best actress. The audience sat in silence as the presenter opened the envelope. Jennifer's name was not called. A different actress had won.

Even though Jennifer did not win the Academy Award, she was finding new opportunities. And after several serious roles, she was ready for something different. Luckily, the popular X-Men **franchise** was launching a new movie. *X-Men: First Class* portrayed the famous comic-book characters during their early years, and the filmmakers needed younger actors for the roles.

◄ **Jennifer arrives at the 2011 Academy Awards.**

Jennifer brushed up on the series by watching the first three X-Men movies. She studied the actress who portrayed the blue, shape-shifting character known as Mystique. If Jennifer was going to play a younger version of Mystique, she needed to know everything about the character.

Her research paid off. Jennifer got the part, and she joined one of Hollywood's largest franchises. "It is huge, but the movies are fantastic and I watched them and became a huge fan," she said.[1]

Jennifer's role as Mystique was difficult. She had to wait patiently while makeup artists painted her entire body blue. The process took up to eight hours. To pass the time, Jennifer played with her phone and cracked jokes with the makeup artists.

"There are actresses who build themselves, and then there are actresses who are built by others. I want to build myself."[2]

—Jennifer Lawrence

▲ Jennifer, in her role as Mystique, faces off against a villain known as Apocalypse.

At the start of the day, she was simply Jennifer. But when the artists were done, she was Mystique.

Jennifer Lawrence was finally a Hollywood star, but she wasn't done yet. Her next big role would make her a superstar.

Chapter 3

LET THE GAMES BEGIN

*H*unger Games director Gary Ross was auditioning women for the starring role of Katniss Everdeen. He knew he wanted more than just another actress. He wanted someone special who could bring the athleticism, determination, and caring that the role required. When Jennifer auditioned, he knew he'd found his Katniss.

"I'd never seen an audition that good. Ever," he said. "She stunned me with the emotional depth of the audition."[3] To prepare for the role, Jennifer needed to get into great physical condition. Though she was athletic growing up, she still needed to work hard.

◄ **Jennifer attends the premiere of *The Hunger Games*, the movie that made her a superstar.**

She trained with stunt professionals. She learned to shoot a bow and arrow, run through rugged woods, and climb trees.

Jennifer didn't let Ross down. She won over the fans of the book series with the emotional way she played Katniss. Her scenes varied. She was sweet and emotional when caring for her family. She was tough and ferocious when forced to fight. Whether she was shooting arrows or holding her little sister's hand, Jennifer brought Katniss to life on the big screen. She even won a Critics' Choice Movie Award.

The Hunger Games and its three sequels became one of the most successful franchises in movie history. Thanks to The Hunger Games, Jennifer was now a Hollywood superstar. She was eager to move into more challenging roles.

"I'm always finding myself drawn to strong characters, probably because I want to be like that."[4]

—Jennifer Lawrence

▲ Jennifer's skills with a bow and arrow made her *Hunger Games* character more believable.

Chapter 4

STILL HUNGRY

The moment Jennifer had been waiting for all evening was finally here. It was the 2013 Academy Awards, and the nominees for Best Actress in a Leading Role were being presented. Jennifer watched the presenter closely as the envelope was cracked open.

She could hardly believe it when her name was announced. She had won! She covered her mouth with her hand and made her way toward the stage. As she climbed the steps to the stage, her foot got caught in her long, white gown. She tripped and fell.

After picking herself up, she made her way to the podium. She clutched her award. Then she looked out at the crowd. They were giving her a standing ovation.

◄ **Jennifer beams as she clutches her Academy Award.**

"You guys are just standing up because you feel bad that I fell," she joked.[5]

Jennifer has come a long way from her horse farm in Kentucky. Many critics consider her one of the best actresses in Hollywood. She has even started to produce and direct movies. Jennifer Lawrence is likely to be a familiar name for many years to come.

THINK ABOUT IT

- If you could play the leading role in a movie based on a book, what would it be?
- Would you rather play a part in an extremely popular movie or win an award for a great performance in an indie film? Why?
- What would you do to stay entertained for eight hours while artists painted you blue for the role of Mystique?

◀ Jennifer and costar Josh Hutcherson press their hands into wet concrete. This ceremony is a tradition for Hollywood stars.

GLOSSARY

Academy Awards (uh-KAD-uh-mee uh-WARDZ): Academy Awards are prizes for the best work in movies. Jennifer has been nominated for several Academy Awards.

agent (AY-juhnt): An agent is a person who arranges jobs for people. Jennifer wanted an agent who would find acting jobs for her.

auditioned (aw-DISH-uhnd): Someone who auditioned has tried out for a part in a performance. Jennifer auditioned for the Mystique role after studying old *X-Men* movies.

franchise (FRAN-chize): A franchise is a series of several works based on one original work. The Hunger Games franchise has four movies.

indie movies (IN-dee MOO-veez): Indie movies, or independent movies, are movies that are not made by large companies. Jennifer got her start acting in indie movies.

nominated (NAH-muh-nay-ted): Nominated means chosen as a finalist for an award. Jennifer has been nominated for many awards.

producer (pruh-DOOS-ur): A producer is a person in charge of making movies. Jennifer auditioned with a producer for *The Hunger Games*.

sequels (SEE-kwuhlz): Sequels are books or movies that continue the story of an earlier work. *The Hunger Games* has had multiple sequels.

SOURCE NOTES

1. Eric Ditzian. "'X-Men' Star Jennifer Lawrence Was Intimidated by 'Gorgeous' Rebecca Romijn." *MTV News*. Viacom International, 20 May 2011. Web. 26 Jan. 2017.

2. "Jennifer Lawrence: Quotes." *IMDB*. IMDB.com, n.d. Web. 26 Jan. 2017.

3. Eric Ditzian. "'Hunger Games' Star Jennifer Lawrence's Audition Best 'Ever,' Director Says." *MTV News*. Viacom International, 12 Mar. 2012. Web. 26 Jan. 2017.

4. Peter Lesser. "'The Hunger Games: Catching Fire' Movie: New Poster Features a Fierce Katniss; Jennifer Lawrence Talks about Her Role." *Latinos Post*. Latinos Post, 14 May 2013. Web. 26 Jan. 2017.

5. "39 of the Best Jennifer Lawrence Quotes of All Time." *Marie Claire*. Time, Inc. (U.K.) Ltd., 4 Nov. 2016. Web. 26 Jan. 2017.

TO LEARN MORE

Books

Aloian, Molly. *Jennifer Lawrence.* New York, NY: Crabtree Publishing Company, 2013.

Morreale, Marie. *Jennifer Lawrence.* New York, NY: Children's Press, 2015.

Web Sites

Visit our Web site for links about Jennifer Lawrence:

childsworld.com/links

Note to Parents, Teachers, and Librarians: We routinely verify our Web links to make sure they are safe and active sites. So encourage your readers to check them out!

INDEX